Main βETA Hu!

Stuck in The Time-Loop

Arjun Pitcher

Preface

You have been ordinary your whole life. Ordinary in a way that no one notices but everyone assumes.

The air was thick with the smell of fresh-cut grass, and the occasional cheer of kids playing kickball drifted over fences. You were the quiet one, sitting on the front stoop, watching the game. Not because you weren't invited, but because you weren't particularly good—or bad—at anything. The game carried on without much difference whether you were in it or not.

At school, you were never the first to raise your hand. Your test scores were decent, never outstanding. Your friends—if you could call them that—floated in and out of your orbit, as easily forgotten as you were included. Teachers, coaches, even neighbors often struggled to recall your name, their eyes flickering with faint recognition before moving on to someone else more memorable.

In high school, while others discovered their "thing"—sports, drama, debate—you wandered the halls, an observer of others' lives. You tried a few clubs, signed up for the yearbook team one semester, even joined a short-lived band as the guy who held the tambourine. But you always faded out, replaced without ceremony.

You are now a man, older but carrying the same unremarkable existence like a well-worn jacket. Your job is unassuming—a back-office clerk in a mid-sized corporation. Days blur into weeks, as you shuffle papers, fill spreadsheets, and navigate the coffee machine with a practiced indifference. Your colleagues greet you politely but forget your birthday. You never mind; it spares you the awkwardness of being the center of attention.

Today, however, something feels... off. It's not the weather—it's just as gray and indifferent as usual. Not the coffee either—it's lukewarm and stale, just like every day. There's a hum, a faint pull, a whisper of something strange in the air.

You step out of your cubicle. The fluorescent lights flicker above, their hum loud in the near-silence of the office. For a brief moment, the ordinary feels unfamiliar, like looking at your reflection in a warped mirror.

If you feel this way, then it is for you. This is my story from my school days before I graduated from school in 2011 (with a hint of sci-fi added to it). The ordinary guy (Arjun) since beginning. Main Beta hu (β).

— Arjun Pitcher
Instagram Handle -
PENNPLOT_PRODUCTION

Table of Content

Chapter – 1 Fumbling in 10th Standard

The memory of that day remained seared into Arjun's mind, a vivid chapter from his teenage years when hope and humiliation collided. It was a warm spring afternoon in 10th grade. The school courtyard buzzed with the chatter of students during recess. Arjun had spent weeks mustering the courage to confess his feelings to Shilpa, the radiant, effortlessly confident girl who seemed to brighten every room she entered.

She was out of his league, and he knew it. Shilpa wasn't just pretty; she had an aura—a magnetic pull that turned heads wherever she went. Her laugh rang out like music in the air, her bold, unapologetic attitude making her the center of attention without even trying. She wasn't cruel, though; once or twice, she'd smiled at Arjun in passing or exchanged a cheerful "Hi" when borrowing his notes. Those fleeting moments had been enough to plant the seed of his crush and fuel his dreams.

That day, clutching a hastily scribbled note in his clammy hands, Arjun approached her while she was not surrounded by her friends. His heart pounded in his chest, his throat dry despite rehearsing the words countless times in front of the mirror.

"Sh-Shilpa," he stammered, his voice barely above a whisper.

She looked up from her conversation, surprised. "Yes, Arjun?" she said, her tone light and kind.

"I...I like you," he managed, the words tumbling out in a rush. "I mean... more than like you. I...I think you're amazing."

Her expression softened, and for a moment, there was silence. Then, as Arjun stood there, clutching the note, her lips twitched. She fought to suppress a giggle—more out of surprise than malice—but the effort showed.

Arjun noticed it. His ears burned, and the note trembled in his hand. "I...I'm sorry," he muttered, retreating before she could say anything. Her friends exchanged knowing glances, and though she called out, "Wait, Arjun," her voice was drowned out by the ringing bell signaling the end of recess.

From that day forward, Arjun's interactions with Shilpa dwindled to polite nods in the hallway. She went on, as she always had, her laughter and confidence unshaken, while Arjun retreated further into himself. He buried himself in books and kept to the edges of social circles, the sting of rejection eroding his self-confidence.

Shilpa, bold and unbothered, moved on as though nothing had happened. Life seemed effortless for her, filled with moments of joy and attention from those around her. Arjun, however, carried the weight of that day like a heavy stone, shaping the years that followed.

But life is long, and this story doesn't end here.

The unraveling of Arjun and Aarav's friendship began subtly, as most deep fractures do. What had started as an easy bond of shared laughs and mutual interests—debating WWE champions, swapping notes, and passing time watching matches—began to fade into a growing chasm during their 11th standard.

Saumya entered the picture like a queen stepping into a palace. She was a girl whose beauty and confidence captivated everyone. Untouchable, magnetic, and seemingly above it all, Saumya was the kind of person whose presence alone shifted dynamics in a room. Arjun, like everyone else, was entranced. He admired her from a distance, weaving quiet fantasies where she might one day notice him.

But it wasn't Arjun she noticed—it was Aarav. His funny, effortless charm and knack for connecting with people drew her in. It started innocently, with brief conversations at the back of the classroom. Soon, the two of them were talking during breaks, texting late into the night, and sharing laughs in ways that seemed alien to Arjun. Their budding relationship became official not long after, and suddenly Aarav was no longer the same person to Arjun.

Aarav began skipping their usual WWE debates to hang out with Saumya and her clique, the "cool crowd." Movie nights and hangouts with Arjun became rare, then nonexistent. When Arjun called, Aarav's responses were short, distracted. "Sorry, bro, I have plans with Saumya. Next time, okay?"

There was no next time. Each ignored call or casual brush-off felt like a splinter driving deeper into Arjun's heart. The jealousy Arjun initially felt toward Aarav was small—a pang of envy at seeing his friend achieve what he had always dreamed of: a connection with a girl like Saumya. But as time passed, that envy twisted into something darker. It wasn't just about Saumya anymore; it was about Aarav leaving him behind, choosing a life and a crowd that didn't include Arjun.

Arjun's resentment grew in silence, feeding on every slight—real or imagined. He began to see Aarav as selfish, a user who had taken his help with studies only to abandon him when he no longer needed it. The betrayal felt personal. Arjun wanted to say something, to call Aarav out, but the words never came. He withdrew instead, retreating into himself, his fantasies of Saumya now tinged with bitterness.

By the time school ended, their friendship was a ghost of what it once was. They barely spoke during farewell events, and after graduation, they went their separate ways. Aarav and Saumya stayed together, their relationship growing stronger. Social media became a cruel mirror for Arjun, reflecting the life Aarav was living—a life Arjun had once dreamed of. Saumya's radiant posts, their romantic dates, the vacations they took together—it all felt like salt in a wound.

Years later, when Aarav and Saumya got married, the news reached Arjun through mutual friends. He didn't attend the wedding. He couldn't. The hatred he had nurtured for Aarav made it impossible to wish him well, even after all these years. It wasn't just about losing a friend anymore—it was about losing the version of life Arjun had built in his head, a version where he was the one with the confidence, the girl, the happy ending.

Now, as an adult, Arjun carries that baggage, the weight of jealousy and betrayal still heavy on his shoulders. But the world hasn't stopped moving.

Chapter – 3 Mistook her Noble Intentions for Love

A Budding Friendship in 11th Grade

In 11th standard, Arjun found himself drawn to Sana, a girl in his class whose beauty, intellect, and humor set her apart from everyone else. Sana wasn't just pretty—she was magnetic, with a personality that made her effortlessly likable. She was witty, approachable, and carried herself with a quiet confidence. To Arjun, she seemed like the perfect blend of brains and charm.

Sana didn't run in Arjun's social circle, but they began to connect through small, genuine moments. It started during math class. Arjun was a little better at math than most of his peers and loved teasing those who struggled, though in a friendly way. Sana, despite her brilliance, would occasionally stumble on tough problems, and Arjun, ever eager to help, would step in with playful jabs.

"Stuck again, Sana? Want me to solve it for you?" he'd tease, smirking.

"Don't get cocky, Arjun. I'll figure it out!" she'd retort with mock annoyance, though a smile always followed.

These exchanges became a routine, and over time, their banter deepened into actual conversations. Sana shared Arjun's love for WWE, a niche interest that most girls in their class dismissed. Arjun would often bring her the latest updates about matches, predictions about upcoming championships, and even humorous anecdotes from the wrestling world. Sana laughed, genuinely enjoying his company.

One afternoon, during a particularly noisy break between classes, Arjun sat at his desk, flipping through his notes. Behind him, Sana was chatting animatedly with a friend. Suddenly, mid-conversation, she leaned on Arjun's shoulder for support, balancing herself casually as she continued talking. It was a fleeting moment, but for Arjun, it felt significant.

In that small gesture, he found comfort. It reassured him that, despite their differences in social circles, Sana saw him as someone she could lean on—literally and figuratively. Arjun felt a spark of hope, a quiet but growing belief that their connection might mean something more.

Dreams of Something More

As their conversations continued, Arjun's mind began to wander. He started imagining what it would be like to date Sana. They shared so many interests, and their chemistry felt natural. Even though Sana was part of the "cool crowd" that included Saumya, Aarav, and Arjun's own cousin brother, she still took the time to talk to him [Arjun]. To Arjun, this was proof that she was different—someone who could see beyond the superficial.

Arjun's thoughts weren't just about Sana, though. He also saw their potential relationship as a bridge to something bigger. Being with Sana could mean gaining access to the "cool group," a clique he had always admired from a distance. He fantasized about being included in their plans, their inside jokes, and their carefree camaraderie. With Sana by his side, he thought, he could finally be part of something he had longed for but never felt he belonged to.

The Disappointment

One day, Arjun overheard the cool crowd planning a day out after school. It was an exciting plan—a movie, followed by snacks at a trendy café. As he listened to their conversation from a distance, he felt a pang of longing. He didn't expect an invitation from Saumya, Aarav, or even his cousin—they rarely included him in their plans. But deep down, he hoped Sana would remember him. After all, they had been talking so much lately. If anyone would think to call him, it would be her.

The day passed, and no invitation came. Arjun waited, checking his phone occasionally, but there were no messages. He was hurt, though he tried to brush it off. "Maybe she forgot," he told himself. But the thought lingered: *Did she ever think of me at all?*

For days after, Arjun wrestled with his emotions. He felt betrayed, but more than that, he felt invisible. He had believed Sana cared enough about him to include him, even if just as a friend. Her silence shattered that illusion.

The Crushing Truth

A few days later, unable to hold back his curiosity, Arjun asked his cousin about the outing. "How was the trip?" he inquired casually, masking the ache in his voice.

"It was great," his cousin replied with a grin, recounting the fun they had.

Arjun hesitated before asking, "Did anyone mention me? Did anyone say I should've been there?"

His cousin paused, his expression softening into one of pity. "No one really brought you up," he admitted. "But... I did. I told them you should've been invited."

Arjun's heart lifted momentarily before his cousin added, "But Sana said, 'Why should we call him? He's not part of the group.'"

Those words struck Arjun like a blow. Of all people, Sana—the one person he thought understood him—had dismissed him so easily. Her words weren't just a rejection; they were a confirmation of his worst fears: that he didn't belong, that he was invisible to the people he admired most.

The Aftermath

Arjun couldn't shake the sting of Sana's words. Slowly, he began to withdraw from her. He stopped teasing her in math class, stopped sharing WWE updates, and stopped initiating conversations. It wasn't a dramatic fallout; it was a quiet fade. Sana, absorbed in her own life and the cool crowd, didn't seem to notice the change.

By the end of school, they had drifted apart completely. Sana moved on, graduating with her usual confidence and charm, while Arjun carried the weight of her words into his adult life.

Years Later

Years passed, and Arjun stumbled across Sana's Instagram profile. She had moved to Germany, building a life of dreams—successful career, vibrant social life, and a string of adventures. Her posts radiated happiness and fulfillment. Arjun felt a mix of emotions: pride that she had achieved so much, but also a lingering ache.

Every time he saw her posts, he couldn't help but remember her words: *"Why should we call him? He's not part of the group."* They echoed in his mind, a painful reminder of a rejection he had never fully healed from.

Even now, as he sits scrolling through her photos, he wonders: *Did I ever mean anything to her? Did she ever think of me?*

It's a question that haunts him, leaving him torn between moving on and holding onto the past.

Chapter – 4 Teachers light the way, but even guiding stars can falter

Arjun had always admired the small joys of life, finding meaning in the connections he built, even when they seemed one-sided. During his 11th and 12th standards, accounts classes became his sanctuary, a place where he felt he could excel. It wasn't just the subject; it was the man who taught it—Abhinav Sir. A new addition to the school faculty, Abhinav Sir had a charm that captivated everyone. He wasn't just a teacher; he was a personality, a presence that lit up the room the moment he walked in.

Girls adored him for his charisma, often giggling at his jokes and hanging on his words. The boys, too, found him approachable and fun, appreciating his knack for blending humor with learning. His teaching was transformative; he made even the driest topics seem engaging. Arjun was no exception—he admired Abhinav Sir deeply, not just for his teaching but for the effortless way he built relationships with students.

However, Arjun soon noticed a pattern that dampened his admiration. Despite his own discipline and dedication—attending every class, participating earnestly—Abhinav Sir seemed to gravitate toward the "cool kids." The naughty ones, who skipped assignments and pulled pranks, somehow became his favorites. They joked with him during lectures, got away with mischief, and shared a camaraderie that Arjun could never hope to replicate.

For Arjun, this was a bitter pill to swallow. He couldn't understand why his efforts went unnoticed. He admired Abhinav Sir so much, yet felt like an afterthought in his eyes. But Arjun didn't let his disappointment fester; he decided to take a lighthearted approach to win his teacher's attention.

The Birthday Plan

When Arjun learned that Abhinav Sir's birthday was approaching, he came up with an idea to make the day memorable—not just for the teacher, but for the whole class. Discussing the plan with his cousin, he proposed a humorous gesture: each boy in the class would bring a rose and present it to Abhinav Sir. It would be a playful reversal of the norm, where girls typically gave roses to teachers. The idea wasn't just funny—it was a way to express appreciation while lightening the mood.

His cousin loved the plan and agreed immediately. Together, they bought the roses, carefully ensuring there was one for every boy in the class. On the big day, the excitement was palpable. Arjun distributed the roses, instructing everyone to play along. When Abhinav Sir entered the classroom, he was met with an unprecedented sight: a line of boys, each holding a rose, waiting to present it to him.

The class erupted in laughter as the roses piled up on Abhinav Sir's desk. The usually composed teacher couldn't contain his amusement. His face lit up with genuine joy, and he laughed heartily, appreciating the thoughtfulness and humor of the gesture. For Arjun, seeing the delight on Abhinav

Sir's face was a moment of triumph. He felt that, finally, he had done something to connect with the teacher he so admired.

The Disappointment

Then came the pivotal moment. Amid the laughter and cheer, Abhinav Sir, curious and excited, asked, "Who planned all this? Who's the mastermind?" His tone was playful, eager to discover the person behind the prank so he could share a laugh with them.

Arjun's cousin, beaming with pride, pointed to Arjun. "It was Arjun's idea!" he announced, expecting applause or at least an engaging exchange.

All eyes turned to Arjun. He felt a rush of anticipation, ready to finally have his moment of recognition. But instead of the lively reaction he'd hoped for, Abhinav Sir simply glanced at him, offered a faint, almost dismissive smile, and moved on to resume the class.

For Arjun, the shift in tone was unmistakable. It was as if the revelation that the idea had come from "ordinary Arjun" had drained the excitement from the moment. Arjun had imagined that Abhinav Sir would laugh, ask questions, and share a connection with him like he did with the cool kids. Instead, it felt like his effort was brushed aside, unworthy of further attention.

That day, Arjun realized the truth: no matter how much he admired Abhinav Sir, the feeling wasn't mutual. He wasn't one of the favorites, wasn't someone who mattered enough to be noticed beyond the surface.

The Lingering Memory

The disappointment stayed with Arjun long after school ended. He never forgot the joy he felt when planning the prank or the excitement of seeing it unfold successfully. But that joy was forever overshadowed by the sting of being overlooked.

As an adult, Arjun occasionally reflects on his school days. The memory of Abhinav Sir—his charisma, his brilliance, his ability to light up a room—is now tainted by the realization that he never saw Arjun as more than a background character.

Scrolling through old pictures or hearing the name "Abhinav Sir" in passing, Arjun feels a pang of bitterness. It's not anger, but a sense of rejection that still lingers. The man he once admired so deeply never reciprocated even a fraction of that admiration. To this day, that memory leaves a bad taste in Arjun's mouth, a reminder of how much it hurts to care for someone who doesn't care back.

And yet, life moves forward.

Chapter – 5 The Story of Arjun, Lakshita, Pari, and Ashutosh

By the time Arjun reached 12th grade, he had grown accustomed to the sting of being overlooked. His experiences with Aarav, Sana, and even Abhinav Sir had left him wounded, but not entirely broken. He still harbored hope for meaningful connections. It was during math classes that he found solace in a small, unexpected group: Lakshita, Pari, Ashutosh, and himself.

This group of four emerged organically, drawn together by shared desks and a common struggle to untangle complex equations. Arjun and Ashutosh sat together at the back, while Lakshita and Pari occupied the row in front. Their dynamic quickly became a highlight of Arjun's day. Between solving problems and scribbling notes, the four of them would chat and share laughs, creating a bond that felt warm and uncomplicated.

For Arjun, these moments became a refuge from the disappointments of the past. He cherished the camaraderie, especially with Ashutosh, who shared his sense of humor and lightheartedness. Lakshita's bubbly personality and Pari's charm added a special spark to their group.

The Hidden Crush

As their friendship grew, Arjun found himself secretly drawn to Pari. She was everything he admired—charming, good-looking, and effortlessly engaging. Arjun never shared his feelings with anyone; he was content to bask in the joy of their group interactions. Yet, as time passed, he began to notice a subtle shift. Ashutosh, too, seemed to develop feelings for Pari, though it happened much later than Arjun's.

Ashutosh's attention toward Pari became more pronounced. During math classes, Ashutosh started pulling lighthearted pranks on Pari—

teasing her, cracking jokes, and making her laugh hysterically. Arjun tried to mimic Ashutosh's playful energy, hoping to elicit the same response from Pari. But when Arjun tried, her reactions were muted, polite at best. Meanwhile, Ashutosh's antics seemed to brighten her day, her laughter coming easily and freely.

It was in these moments that Arjun began to feel invisible, a shadow in the group he once cherished. Lakshita and Pari's close friendship flourished, while Ashutosh became the clear focus of Pari's attention. Arjun felt like the odd one out, an unremarkable presence in a group that had brought him so much happiness.

The Birthday Disappointment

Arjun's birthday was approaching, and he saw it as an opportunity to reclaim a sense of belonging. He decided to invite Ashutosh, Lakshita, and Pari to celebrate with him at a mall. He imagined a perfect day where the group's attention—especially Pari's—would be on him. It was his day, after all. For once, he allowed himself to dream that things might go his way.

When the day arrived, Arjun dressed with care, excitement bubbling in his chest. At the mall, the group met up, and for a brief moment, everything seemed perfect. But as the hours unfolded, Arjun's excitement turned to dismay.

Rather than focusing on Arjun, the group dynamic shifted almost immediately. Ashutosh and Pari spent the majority of the time talking to each other, their chemistry undeniable. They clicked pictures together, exchanged inside jokes, and seemed oblivious to the fact that it was Arjun's birthday. Lakshita tried to include Arjun in conversation occasionally, but even she was drawn to the vibrant energy between Ashutosh and Pari.

Arjun felt sidelined, a mere spectator at his own celebration. What was supposed to be a special day for him had turned into a showcase of Ashutosh and Pari's growing connection. He smiled through the pain, but inside, he felt betrayed.

The Drift

The birthday experience marked a turning point for Arjun. He could no longer find joy in the group. Sitting with them in math class became unbearable, each session a reminder of his place on the periphery. Eventually, he stopped sitting with them altogether. He began skipping casual chats, choosing instead to focus on his studies or sit in solitude.

To his shock, no one seemed to notice his absence. Lakshita, Pari, and Ashutosh continued their lives as if nothing had changed. The bonds that had once felt so meaningful to Arjun seemed fragile and one-sided.

The Aftermath

After school ended, the group dissolved. Ashutosh moved to Australia, married, and built a new life. He never reached out to Arjun again, not even for a friendly hello. Lakshita and Pari faded into distant memories, their paths diverging from Arjun's.

Years later, in a moment of nostalgia, Arjun mustered the courage to message Pari on Facebook. Her response was polite but indifferent—a half-hearted "Hi" followed by a brief, generic exchange. It was clear she didn't share the same depth of connection Arjun had once felt. Hurt by her lack of interest, Arjun stopped trying to reach out.

Lingering Pain

As an adult, Arjun occasionally reflects on those days in 12th grade, particularly the group that brought him fleeting joy. He remembers the laughter, the shared moments during math classes, and the hope he had placed in their friendship. But those memories are overshadowed by the way it all unraveled—the way he was ignored on his birthday, the way Pari and Ashutosh grew closer while he faded into the background.

For Arjun, the pain of being overlooked isn't just about the group. It's about the pattern it represents—the repeated sense of being invisible, unimportant, and excluded. Whether it was Aarav, Sana, Abhinav Sir, or this group of four, the outcome always seemed the same.

Now, as he navigates life, Arjun carries these memories like a shadow, a reminder of how much he longed for connection and how often it eluded him. The question that lingers is whether he can let go of these hurts and rebuild his sense of self-worth—or if these moments will continue to haunt him.

Chapter – 6 Main βeta hu

Arjun had grown up and was doing a job. One day, **now in present day [2024]**, he was coming back to home from office at late night. The metro hummed with its usual mechanical rhythm as Arjun leaned against the cold steel pole, his bag slung over one shoulder, his tie loosened from the day's grind. The familiar anonymity of the crowd engulfed him—the hum of muted conversations, the faint music leaking from someone's earphones, and the occasional scrape of a shoe against the floor. The world moved, indifferent as always, while Arjun stood still, lost in his thoughts.

He had spent his life chasing an elusive dream—a sense of belonging, recognition, and value. From school to college, and even in his career, the story was the same. He was the quiet observer, the reliable background figure, never the one who commanded attention or admiration. The scars of those years—being overlooked by friends, rejected by crushes, overshadowed by the so-called "alpha males"—had shaped him, embedding a deep sense of inadequacy that no amount of professional success or personal milestones could erase.

The Pattern of Life

College had been a turning point—or so Arjun thought at the time. He had entered with optimism, fueled by the widely sold idea that lifelong friendships were forged on college campuses. He imagined a fresh start, a chance to be seen and valued for who he truly was. But history repeated itself. Friendships remained surface-level, fleeting connections that fizzled out as quickly as they formed. He watched from the sidelines as the charismatic, outgoing "alpha males" attracted the admiration of peers and the attention of women.

Crushes came and went, each leaving behind a familiar ache. Whenever Arjun gathered the courage to express his feelings, he found himself in the same scenario—rejected or left unnoticed, his words lost in the shadow of someone else's charm. The sting of unrequited affection was compounded by the realization that his quiet demeanor was no match for the confidence and magnetism of those who effortlessly drew people in.

Life Beyond College

After graduating, Arjun threw himself into his studies and became a Chartered Accountant—a goal he had envisioned since his school days. His hard work paid off, landing him a position at a prestigious consultancy firm. He thought that perhaps now, in a professional environment, he would find the meaningful connections that had eluded him. But even here, the pattern persisted.

In the office, the loud, confident voices of his colleagues—the "alpha males"—drew all the attention. They were the ones who charmed clients, engaged effortlessly in team meetings, and became the life of every office gathering. Arjun, despite his talent and dedication, found himself relegated to the background, his contributions overshadowed by others' charisma. He was respected, but rarely celebrated.

Marriage and Personal Life

In time, Arjun's focus shifted to his personal life. He entered into a few relationships, hoping to find someone who could see beyond the walls he had built around himself. But those relationships faltered. His past experiences, the rejections and feelings of inadequacy, had left him guarded and cynical. His partners eventually grew weary of his negativity and inability to embrace life with confidence, and they drifted away.

Finally, Arjun married through an arranged setup. His wife was kind and understanding, and their life together appeared stable and happy from the outside. They built a life of comfort, with a home, vacations, and mutual respect. But within Arjun, the darkness remained. No matter how much he achieved—a thriving career, a stable marriage, financial security—he couldn't shake the feeling that he was still invisible, still the man who faded into the background.

The Breaking Point

On that fateful evening, as the metro carried him home, Arjun found himself overwhelmed by a lifetime of unspoken pain. The hum of the train and the indifferent faces around him seemed to echo his own invisibility. His hands trembled slightly as he gripped the pole, his chest heavy with the weight of years spent trying and failing to feel like he belonged.

His thoughts raced: *Why couldn't I be like them? The ones who light up a room, who people gravitate toward without effort. Why am I always the one left behind?* He thought of Aarav, Sana, Abhinav Sir, Ashutosh, Pari—faces from the past that still haunted him, reminding him of every rejection, every moment he felt small.

In that moment, something inside him broke. Tears welled up in his eyes, but he didn't care if anyone noticed. His voice, trembling with frustration and fatigue, escaped him in a quiet, bitter declaration.

"*Main beta hu...*" he muttered under his breath, then louder, "*Main beta hu!*" His voice cracked with emotion. "*Main alpha nahi hoon. Main kabhi alpha nahi banunga.*" *(I am not an alpha and I never will be one).*

He closed his eyes, feeling the sting of tears rolling down his cheeks. He had finally said it aloud—the thing he had been carrying in silence for years. It wasn't anger or self-pity; it was a raw, painful acceptance. Arjun had spent his entire life measuring himself against a standard he could never meet, chasing a version of himself that didn't exist.

He sank into the realization: *I am not an alpha. I was never meant to be one. I am just... ordinary. A beta. The one who stays in the background, unnoticed.*

Chapter – 7 Twist of Fate

It was an ordinary evening, or so Arjun thought. The metro screeched to a halt at the station, and he stepped out, blending into the sea of commuters making their way home. His mind was still clouded by the events of the day, his emotions raw from finally admitting aloud that he was, in his own words, a "Beta." As he scanned the street for an auto-rickshaw, his shoulders slumped, weighed down by years of disappointment and self-doubt.

The bustling street was alive with noise—a blend of honking cars, vendors shouting their wares, and the hum of life in the city. But amidst the chaos, something unusual happened. A voice cut through the clamor, calm yet commanding.

"Stop. Don't move."

Arjun froze mid-step, the hair on his neck standing on end. Turning around slowly, his eyes widened at the sight of the figure before him. A woman, exuding confidence and danger, stood just a few feet away. She wore a black leather jacket and matching pants that fit her like a second skin. Her dark sunglasses reflected the flickering neon lights of the street, and her hair was tied back with military precision. In her hand was a weapon—a sleek, futuristic-looking laser gun that glowed faintly at its core.

Arjun's heart raced as he stammered, "W-who are you? Why are you pointing that… thing at me?"

The woman didn't lower the gun. Her voice was sharp and authoritative as she said, "My name is Emma. I'm here to arrest Rocky for violating the continuum of time and breaking the rules of time travel."

The Shocking Accusation

Arjun's brow furrowed in confusion. "Time travel? Arrest? Who's Rocky? What are you talking about? You've got the wrong person!"

Emma's lips curled into a small, knowing smirk. "Don't play dumb, Rocky. You can't fool me again, not after the hundred times you've outmaneuvered me. I've been tracking you across the timeline, and now it's over. I'm taking you to the Temporal Guard's time prison. You've run out of tricks."

Arjun's confusion deepened. "I have no idea what you're talking about! My name is Arjun, not Rocky. I'm just an accountant, for God's sake! I've never broken any laws, let alone… time laws?"

But Emma wasn't listening. She stepped closer, her gun aimed directly at his chest. Her movements were precise, calculated, like a predator closing in on its prey.

Chaos and Escape

Just as Emma reached for Arjun, chaos erupted. From a nearby concert venue, a stampede of people surged into the street, panicked and shouting. The crowd swarmed around them, a sea of bodies jostling and pushing. The noise was deafening—shouts, cries, and the thundering of footsteps drowned out everything else.

Emma lost sight of Arjun in the chaos, her grip on her weapon tightening as she scanned the crowd. "Damn it!" she muttered, frustration etched across her face. "Don't think you've won, Rocky. I'll find you again."

Meanwhile, Arjun took advantage of the confusion. His instincts screamed at him to run, and he obeyed without hesitation. Ducking and weaving through the crowd, he put as much distance as possible between himself and the woman with the gun. His heart pounded in his chest, fear and adrenaline propelling him forward.

The Grocery Store Encounter

Eventually, the noise of the crowd faded, and Arjun found himself in a quieter part of the street. His breaths came in ragged gasps as he leaned against a lamppost, trying to make sense of what had just happened. "Who was she? And why was she calling me Rocky?" he murmured to himself.

His eyes fell on a small grocery store nearby, its warm lights a stark contrast to the chaos he'd just escaped. Seeking a moment to collect himself, he stepped inside.

The store clerk, a young man busy at the billing counter, looked up as Arjun entered. "Arjun, right?" he said casually.

Arjun froze. "What? How do you know my name?"

The clerk didn't answer directly. Instead, with a very scared emotions and expressions, he nodded toward a staircase leading to the basement. "Someone's waiting for you downstairs. They said you'd come."

Arjun's stomach twisted in knots. "What? Who's waiting for me? What's going on?"

The clerk simply gestured toward the basement. "Go see for yourself."

Despite the fear gnawing at him, curiosity—and perhaps a strange sense of destiny—drove Arjun forward. He descended the narrow staircase, each step creaking under his weight. The basement was dimly lit, the air thick with the scent of dust and mildew.

At the far end of the room, a figure stood in the shadows. Arjun squinted, trying to make out the details. As he moved closer, the figure stepped forward into the light.

The Doppelgänger

Arjun's breath hitched. Standing before him was a man—his exact double. But this version of himself was strikingly different. The man was taller, more muscular, with sharp, confident features that seemed to belong to a movie star or an action hero. His clothes were rugged and practical, though torn and bloodstained. Blood dripped from a gash on his forehead, and his left shoulder was bruised and battered.

"Hello, sir!" the man said with a crooked grin, his voice carrying an unsettling familiarity. "Rocky, reporting for duty!"

Arjun took a step back, his mind reeling. "What the… Who the hell are you? How is this possible? You… you look like me!"

The man chuckled, wiping the blood from his mouth. "That's because I *am* you. Sort of. Name's Rocky. I'm Arjun… but from a distant future."

Arjun's eyes widened in disbelief. "Future? Time travel? What's going on? This has to be a prank!"

Rocky shook his head. "It's no prank, my friend. It's your life. And it's about to get a whole lot crazier."

Chapter – 8 The Battle: Part-1

Arjun's world spun as he tried to comprehend the impossible truth before him. Who was this version of himself? What had he done to attract the wrath of Emma and the Temporal Guard? And most importantly, what did this mean for the ordinary, "Beta" life he thought he had resigned himself to?

One thing was certain: Arjun's life would never be the same.

Rocky leaned back against the wall, his grin both charming and infuriating. Despite his injuries, he carried himself with an unshakable confidence that Arjun couldn't help but envy. Rocky raised a hand, signaling Arjun to calm down as his barrage of questions poured out.

"Whoa, whoa, slow down, champ," Rocky said, his voice dripping with wit. "I get it. You're confused, you're scared, and—let me guess—you're wondering if you've gone completely insane. I'd probably feel the same way if I were… well, me."

Arjun, still shaken, couldn't hold back. "What the hell is going on? Who are you? Why do you look like me? What's this nonsense about time travel? And why is someone trying to arrest *me*?"

Rocky chuckled, brushing some dirt off his ripped sleeve. "Okay, okay. Let's start with the basics, shall we? First of all, yes, I look like you because I *am* you. Sort of. I'm Arjun… from the future. A version of you that decided to break a few rules, have some fun, and, uh, let's just say, rewrite the script of life a little."

Arjun's mouth hung open, his brain struggling to keep up. "Rewrite? What does that even mean?"

Rocky smirked. "Let me put it this way. You know that whole 'Beta' thing you've been wallowing in? That whole sob story about being invisible, overlooked, and stuck in the background while the 'Alpha males' steal the spotlight? Yeah, I lived that too buddy. But one day, this day, I decided I'd had enough. I wasn't going to accept being a 'Beta' anymore. So, I made a choice—an outrageous, insane, life-changing choice."

Arjun frowned, his curiosity piqued despite his fear. "What choice?"

Rocky stepped forward, his tone growing serious. "I stole a piece of technology. A little something that let me travel through time. And with it, I rewrote my life. I changed events, seized opportunities, and built the kind of life we've always dreamed of. I became the guy everyone notices. The guy people look up to. The Alpha."

Rocky leaned against the wall, his face a mix of nostalgia and weariness as he began recounting the story, his voice steady and deliberate.

"Arjun," he said, "185 years ago, I was standing right where you are now—confused, scared, and with a thousand questions running through my mind. My life up until that point had been almost exactly like yours: full of disappointments, rejections, and feeling invisible. And then, out of nowhere, my future self walked into my life, just like I'm standing here in front of you today."

Arjun blinked, his confusion deepening. "So… what you're saying is that this has all happened before? You've been me, and someone else was you?"

Rocky nodded, a faint smile tugging at his lips. "Exactly. My future self—let's call him the *First Rocky*—looked just like me but older, more battle-worn. He calmed me down, just like I'm calming you down now, and he told me the story, just like I'm telling it to you. And then, he said the words that changed everything: 'I'm passing on the Temporal Key to you.'"

Arjun's eyes widened. "The… Temporal Key? You mean the watch? Why would he do that?"

Rocky's expression grew somber. "Because his time had come. He told me that he'd lived for 205 years—205 years of being an Alpha, living like a king, bending the rules of time, and running from the Temporal Guard. But he knew his luck had run out. He told me the Temporal Guard was closing in, and this time, there would be no escape. He accepted it, Arjun. He accepted that he would die that day. And because he knew his end was near, he wanted to pass the watch to me—to give me the same chance he had, to rewrite my story."

The Battle of the First Rocky

Arjun stared at Rocky in disbelief. "He… accepted it? He just accepted that he was going to die?"

Rocky nodded, his voice heavy with emotion. "Yes. It shocked me too. I couldn't believe it. I asked him, just like you're asking me now: 'You're really okay with this? You've accepted that you're going to die?' And he looked me in the eye and said, 'Yes, I've lived my life to the fullest, and now it's your turn.'"

Arjun's heart raced as he tried to process this. "So, what happened? Did they… did the Temporal Guard come for him?"

Rocky took a deep breath. "They came. It wasn't long after he finished telling me his story. The Guard burst into the godown, armed with their futuristic weapons, their eyes set on him—on the First Rocky. He knew they would come, but he wasn't about to go down without a fight. He told me to stay back, to stay safe, and then he charged at them like the warrior he had become."

Arjun's chest tightened. "Did he… win?"

Rocky shook his head. "No. He fought valiantly, taking down several guards with him, but they were too many, too prepared. One of their lasers [referring to Emma] hit him square in the forehead. I still remember the moment it happened—the way he fell to the ground, lifeless. The man who had once been me, who had lived like a god, was gone in an instant."

A Second Chance

Arjun's voice trembled as he asked, "But… didn't they kill you too? I mean, wouldn't they think you were just as guilty?"

Rocky's expression softened. "No, they didn't. You see, at that time, I hadn't committed any crimes. I hadn't tampered with time, hadn't broken the laws of the continuum. They realized I was innocent—just a younger version of the man they were after. After they confirmed that, they decided to leave me alone. One of the guards even stayed behind to prepare a report and ensure the First Rocky's body was taken away properly. He told me I'd be escorted back home safely."

Arjun's brow furrowed. "Then… what happened? If they were going to let you go, how did you end up with the watch?"

A sly grin spread across Rocky's face. "That's where things got interesting. While the sole soldier was busy filing his report and preparing the body, I saw my chance. I reached for the First Rocky's wrist, slipped the Temporal Key—the watch—off his arm, and activated it. The soldier didn't even realize what was happening until it was too late. In a flash of light, I disappeared, traveling far into the future."

Arjun stared, speechless. "You… you just took it? You time-traveled? Just like that?"

Rocky shrugged, his grin widening. "What can I say? Desperate times call for desperate measures. And that, Arjun, is how I became the next Rocky. The rest, as they say, is history. Now, it's your turn to decide."

A Fork in the Road

Arjun's mind raced, his heart pounding in his chest. Everything he had just heard felt like a story ripped straight from a science fiction movie. But the man standing before him—the future version of himself—was proof that it was real.

Rocky placed a hand on Arjun's shoulder, his voice low and steady. "Arjun, this isn't just a story. This is your life now. The Temporal Guard will come for me soon, just like they came for the First Rocky. I have lived my life and am prepared to die because today I will die. And when they do come, you'll have a choice to make: to walk away, or to take the watch from my corpse and rewrite your destiny. I won't lie to you—it's a dangerous path, filled with risks and sacrifices. But it's also a chance to become something more.

To break free of the life you've always felt trapped in."

Arjun swallowed hard, the weight of the decision pressing down on him. "What if I don't want to take it? What if I just want to live my ordinary life?"

Rocky smiled faintly. "Then you'll go back to your life, just as it is. And there's nothing wrong with that. But if you've ever felt like you were meant for something greater... now's your chance."

As Rocky's words hung in the air, a faint rumble echoed from above. The sound of heavy boots and mechanical hums grew louder, closer. The Temporal Guard was coming.

Rocky turned to Arjun, his expression resolute. "Time's almost up. What will you do, Arjun?"

Arjun, still overwhelmed by the chaos of the situation, had one last question burning in his mind. He hesitated for a moment, then asked, "You said the First Rocky told you he lived for 205 years, but you just said you've only lived for 185 years. Why is there a 20-year gap? What's the difference between his story and yours?"

Rocky's face shifted, his grin softening into a more reflective expression. He crossed his arms and sighed, as though grappling with the complexity of the answer. "Time travel isn't a game, Arjun. It's no joke. When you start breaking the rules of time, when you're constantly rewriting history, the timeline doesn't just sit there like a stone. It's fluid, chaotic. Every action, every small decision, ripples through the continuum. It might not seem like much at first, but over years—decades—those small changes add up."

Arjun frowned, still trying to wrap his head around it. "So, you're saying the timeline… changed? Because of what you did?"

Rocky nodded. "Exactly. Think of it like this: the First Rocky told me his story, and I tried to follow it as closely as I could. But I'm not him. I made different choices along the way—maybe not big ones, but small, discrete actions. A word here, a decision there. It's like walking down a forest path: even if you're trying to retrace someone's footsteps, your own steps will never fall in exactly the same places."

Arjun's eyes widened. "So those small changes… they shaved off 20 years of your life?"

Rocky smirked faintly. "Maybe. Or maybe I just burned out faster. I lived hard, Arjun— sometimes too hard. The point is, the timeline is never static. What I've done in the past 185 years has shifted things just enough that my story turned out differently than the First Rocky's. And if you take the watch and start your journey, your story will be different from mine. You might live longer than me. Or shorter. Who knows?"

Arjun's throat tightened. "Doesn't that scare you? Knowing you've lost 20 years, knowing I might lose even more?"

Rocky's grin returned, sharp and unapologetic. "Scare me? Arjun, I've lived 185 years as an Alpha. That's 185 years of adventures, victories, love, and excitement—far more than the ordinary life I left behind. If I died tomorrow, I'd still say it was worth it." He leaned closer, his voice dropping to a near whisper. "The real question is, how much are *you* willing to risk? How much are you willing to lose… for a chance to truly live?"

Arjun still worried to do this all alone if this version of Rocky dies. Then Arjun asks can't it be possible that we both fight together and both survive and you teach me the cool ways of being an Alpha. Can't we both try to get out of here alive. To this Rocky replied, "*No. It cannot happen. One of us has to die today. It is written. This cannot change. Of all the faults and tricks which we can do to change time, somethings remain constant and one of us dying tonight is that constant. So, my time has come, I will die today and you live for next hundreds of years being an alpha and then similar to me, you pass the torch to next Arjun*". Arjun was trying to soak all this information and was really scared of what will happen next.

Arjun's heart pounded as the sound of the Temporal Guard's approach grew louder. The future, wild and uncertain, loomed before him. One decision, one moment, could change everything—not just for himself, but for the timeline itself.

Rocky stood tall, watching Arjun intently. "So, Arjun," he said, his tone calm but resolute. "Let's see how long *you* manage to live."

The room was a chaotic battlefield. The Temporal Guard soldiers stormed in, their sleek black armor gleaming under the flickering godown lights. Rocky, standing defiantly in the center of the room, gripped his laser gun tightly. His face bore a smirk of defiance, but his eyes were razor-sharp with focus. Arjun, wide-eyed and trembling, ducked behind a worn-out sofa, his breathing shallow as he watched the chaos unfold.

The soldiers encircled Rocky, their weapons raised, laser sights trained on him. "Surrender, Rocky!" one of them barked.

Rocky's smirk deepened. "Surrender?" he said mockingly, raising his weapon. "Sorry, boys, not my style."

He pulled the trigger, sending a searing blue laser bolt into the chest of the closest soldier. The man collapsed with a grunt, his armor sparking as the energy tore through it. The room erupted into chaos. Soldiers fired back, their lasers crisscrossing the dim space. Rocky moved like a dancer in the middle of a violent storm, dodging beams and returning fire with precision.

The Arrival of Emma

Rocky took down two more soldiers, his movements swift and calculated. But as he turned to fire at another target, a familiar voice rang out above the noise.

"Rocky! This ends now!"

Emma entered the room, her black leather jacket gleaming under the fluorescent lights. Her laser gun was raised, her stance firm and commanding.

She moved with the confidence of a seasoned warrior, her every step radiating purpose.

Rocky turned to face her, his grin fading into a grim line. "Emma," he said, his voice low and edged with bitterness. "Right on time."

She didn't hesitate. Emma fired, and Rocky ducked just in time to avoid the blast. He returned fire, but Emma was faster, her agility matching his every move. The two exchanged a flurry of shots, their duel a clash of skill and determination.

Suddenly, Emma sidestepped one of Rocky's blasts and aimed carefully. A single red beam shot from her gun, hitting Rocky square in the chest. He staggered backward, his smirk faltering as pain washed over his face.

Rocky fell to the ground, his laser gun slipping from his grasp and **skidding across the floor—** coming to rest right at the tips of Arjun's toes.

The End of Rocky

The remaining soldiers lowered their weapons, relief washing over them. "We got him," one of them said.

Emma stood over Rocky's lifeless body, her weapon still raised. She exhaled deeply, her voice steady but laced with triumph. "It's over. Rocky is dead."

A higher-ranking officer entered the room, his demeanor stoic. "Congratulations, Emma," he said. "All our sacrifices have led to this moment. The loop is finally broken. Rocky is gone, and no more will follow."

Emma's face hardened, her gaze shifting to Arjun, who was still crouched behind the sofa. Her grip on the gun tightened as she raised it toward him. "What about him?" she said coldly. "He may look innocent now, but we know what happens. This so-called Arjun will rise again. He'll take the watch, and a new Rocky will be born."

The superior raised a hand, stopping her. "No, Emma. He hasn't done anything yet. He's innocent. We cannot kill or imprison an innocent man."

"But you know how this ends!" Emma snapped. "He'll follow the same path, make the same mistakes!"

"Not this time," the superior replied firmly. "We've ended the loop. This was the last Rocky. There will be no more."

The superior stated that he has seen the life of this Arjun. He is different. He is weaker than all the

Rocky's. He is the Beta of all the Betas. He has lived a pitty life and he does not have it in him what other Arjun's, who came before had. Listening all this Arjun's heart sank and he did not understand whether to be happy about it (as they would not arrest him) or feel sad about it (as the superior defined him the weakest version of the Beta's).

Emma, clearly unconvinced with the superior, glared at Arjun and said to him that if you ever tried to do something fishy, I will catch you and kill you in a blink. After threatening Arjun, she obeyed her superior's command, lowering her weapon. The soldiers began to leave. The superior stayed behind for a moment, placing an officer in charge of the investigation and the godown.

The Moment of Choice

The officer who was left behind for the investigation report looked at Arjun with pitty and started joking about him and said "sorry bro. But its ok. Not all can be the Best version of Beta. Some one has to stand at the last of line? Don't you agree". Arjun really got hurt and angry by this insult, but he was helpless as he could not do anything.

As the officer prepared his report, Arjun remained frozen. His mind was a storm of fear and confusion. *Was this really over? Could he just go home and pretend none of this happened?*

The officer glanced at Arjun. "Don't even think about it," he said flatly, his voice dripping with suspicion. "I've seen too many of you Arjuns try to pull the same stunt. I'm watching you, and if you even move toward that watch, I'll have you arrested."

Arjun stared at the lifeless body of Rocky, the watch still strapped to his wrist. *This was my moment,* Arjun thought. *This was supposed to be my destiny. I was meant to take that watch, to live 185 years as an Alpha.*

But the officer's watchful eyes and the weight of his own fear kept him paralyzed. He felt powerless, trapped in the same cycle of hesitation and self-doubt that had plagued him his entire life. *Even among all the versions of me, I'm the weakest Beta,* he thought bitterly.

Then, he noticed something—the faint glint of a laser gun lying near his foot. The weapon Rocky had dropped earlier. Arjun's heart raced. He never used a gun in his entirely life, but this was his only chance. He carefully picked up the gun, hiding it behind his back.

The Breaking Point

Arjun stood and faced the officer, the laser gun trembling in his hand. "Step back," he said, his voice unsteady. "Let me take the watch and leave."

The officer frowned, unimpressed and laughed. He pressed a distress alarm on his wrist device, and a shrill sound filled the room. "You've made the worst decision of your life, kid," the officer said calmly. "Reinforcements are coming, and you're as good as done."

Panicking, Arjun stepped forward, his finger tightening on the trigger. "Don't come any closer!" he shouted.

The officer ignored the warning, advancing steadily. "You don't have it in you, weak Arjun. Just put the gun down."

In a moment of desperation, anger and frustration, Arjun pulled the trigger. A bright beam of energy shot from the gun, hitting the officer square in the head. The man crumpled to the ground, lifeless !!

Arjun stared at the body, his hands shaking. He couldn't believe what he'd done. "What… what have I become?" he whispered.

But there was no time to reflect. He rushed to Rocky's corpse, unstrapping the watch and securing it to his own wrist. The device hummed to life, its screen glowing as Arjun entered the year "2050" in the watch. A swirling portal appeared before him, its light bathing the room in a surreal glow.

As Arjun prepared to step into the portal, another portal opened nearby. Emma emerged answering to the distress call, her gun raised. She looked at the corpse of the investigation officer and was shocked. Then she faced towards Arjun and shouted "Stop, Arjun!". "This isn't you. You don't have to do this!"

Arjun turned to her, with tears in eyes of both joy and anger and then replaced by a calm determination look. He smiled faintly, his eyes meeting hers. "You're wrong, Emma," he said. "This *is* me. It's who I've always wanted to be."

Before Emma could fire, Arjun stepped into the portal. As the light enveloped him, his voice echoed in the room.

"MAIN ALPHA HU!"

And then, he was gone.

About the Author

Arjun Pitcher is a storyteller who weaves tales that blend the mystical with the profoundly human, exploring the complexities of relationships, identity, lust, seduction, bound and desire. Born with an unquenchable curiosity for the extraordinary desires hidden within the ordinary, Arjun Pitcher began writing weaving stories at a young age, captivated by the magic of words and their power to transport readers to worlds both enchanting and unsettling.

Arjun (under the brand of **Pen N Plot Productions**) continues to create narratives that leave a lasting impression, offering readers both escape and reflection. If you loved Arjun's list above, you could also explore his original stories as mentioned below –

Arjun's Library -

1. Manipulation: The Curse of Kisses (2024)
2. The Secret Seller (2024)
3. Top 10 Must Watch Movies: Behind Closed
    Doors (2024)
4. Top 10 Must Watch Movies: Beyond Closed
    Doors (2024)

What's Next

Thank you for joining me on this extraordinary journey through the time loops of *Main Beta Hu*. Arjun's story is one of transformation—of wrestling with rejection, questioning fate, and discovering the power that lies within.

But as you've seen, every choice comes with consequences, and every rise brings its challenges. Arjun's journey is far from over. What happens when the Beta becomes the Alpha? What new battles will he face—not just with others, but within himself?

In the next chapter, **Main Alpha Hu**, we'll dive deeper into the paradoxes of power, the cost of rewriting time, and the ultimate question: Can you escape your own fate?

Stay tuned. The story has only just begun.